CD must be returned with book or
full replacement costs will be
charged.

BLUEGRASS
Breeze

Story

Dan Rhema

Illustration

Michael Leonard

MESQUITE
TREE
PRESS

To my daughters,
Sydel, Kendall and Alexandra.

D. R.

To my mother's art,
father's discipline,
wife's faith.

M. L.

A cool brisk wind carried the news of the new arrival to the far reaches of the farm.

The wind found its way into the barn
and softly, gently welcomed
the newborn colt.

The newborn breathed deeply of the cool sweet air and rose to his feet.

One fine summer day, a warm breeze rippled through the bluegrass and caught the young colt's eye.

The young colt gave a little kick
and began chasing the breeze across the field.

As he felt the brush of the wind through his mane, the yearling understood that this is what he was born to do.

Each morning the colt awoke
knowing that he was growing
closer to his goal - to catch the wind.

Imagine the colt's surprise to find that there was another who loved the feel of the wind in his face as much as he did.

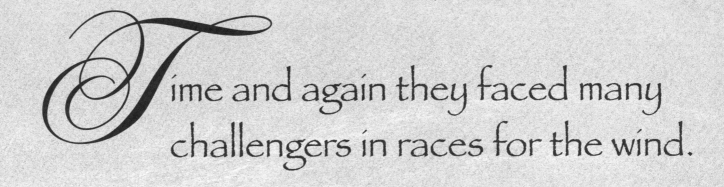

*T*ime and again they faced many challengers in races for the wind.

A warm welcoming wind carried the news of a very special day to the far reaches of the track.

It was a day when the best of the wind chasers were gathered together.

The roar of the crowd drove the powerful horse forward until once again he felt the familiar caress of the wind against his face.

The sound of thundering hooves behind him,
he knew on this day he was closest
to catching the wind.

What does it mean to win – when you are chasing the wind?

Bluegrass Breeze

© 2004 Cymar Music and Mesquite Tree Music
Words and Music by Doris Nance, Jim Peterson Schmitt and Dan Rhema

Cool, spring mornin' the news arrived today about a newborn colt that was born in the hay. Family gathered 'round for the birth at the barn and watched that newborn colt learn to stand on his own.

They call him Bluegrass, Bluegrass, Bluegrass Breeze, raised in Kentucky he's wild and free. Born to be a thoroughbred and to race in the Derby, he's Bluegrass, Bluegrass, Bluegrass Breeze.

Months have passed, seems like summer's here to stay. The breeze is blowin' on this bluegrass day; now's the time for challenges and to win this race as he runs around the track with the wind upon his face.

They call him Bluegrass, Bluegrass, Bluegrass Breeze, raised in Kentucky he's wild and free. Born to be a thoroughbred and to race in the Derby, he's Bluegrass, Bluegrass, Bluegrass Breeze.

This is the day that the world waits to see, with the roar of the crowd as they spring from their seats. Now they reach the finish line and Bluegrass can't be beat with a blanket of roses and petals at his feet.

They call him Bluegrass, Bluegrass, Bluegrass Breeze, raised in Kentucky he's wild and free. Born to be a thoroughbred and win the Derby, he's Bluegrass, Bluegrass, Bluegrass Breeze.

They call him Bluegrass, Bluegrass, Bluegrass Breeze, raised in Kentucky he's wild and free. Born to be a thoroughbred and win the Derby, he's Bluegrass, Bluegrass, Bluegrass Breeze. They call him Bluegrass, Bluegrass Breeze.